Vietnam War Echoes

America Literature 20th century, Volume 2

MICHAEL SMITH

Published by Graywolf Press, 2024.

VIETNAM WAR ECHOES

First edition. May 14, 2024.

ISBN: 979-8224559268

Written by MICHAEL SMITH.

Also by MICHAEL SMITH

America Literature 20th century
Dictatorship Diaries
Vietnam War Echoes

Table of Contents

For those who bravely served, for those who courageously resisted, and for those whose voices echo through the annals of history, this book is dedicated. To the soldiers who fought on distant shores, to the families who bore the weight of their absence, and to the activists who stood up for peace and justice, your sacrifices will never be forgotten. May this book honor your memories, illuminate your stories, and inspire future generations to strive for a world where conflict yields to compassion and reconciliation prevails over division.

Chapter 1: Introduction

Setting the Stage: The Vietnam War, a Conflict of Consequence

The Vietnam War stands as one of the most consequential events in American history, leaving an indelible mark on both the nation's psyche and its global standing. Beginning in the aftermath of World War II, the conflict emerged from the complex interplay of geopolitical tensions, Cold War dynamics, and the struggle for Vietnamese independence. It would come to define a generation, shaping political discourse, social movements, and cultural expressions for decades to come.

The roots of the Vietnam War can be traced back to the early 20th century, when Vietnam was a French colony known as French Indochina. As the wave of decolonization swept across Asia after World War II, Vietnamese nationalists led by Ho Chi Minh sought independence from French rule. However, the Cold War rivalry between the United States and the Soviet Union would soon engulf Vietnam in a larger struggle for influence.

In the aftermath of the Korean War, the United States adopted the containment policy, aimed at preventing the spread of communism. The Domino Theory, popularized by President Dwight D. Eisenhower, posited that the fall of one Southeast Asian nation to communism would lead to the collapse of others, like a row of dominos. This ideological framework would shape American intervention in Vietnam for years to come.

By the late 1950s, the conflict in Vietnam escalated into a full-fledged war between the communist forces of North Vietnam, supported by the Soviet Union and China, and the anti-communist government of South Vietnam, backed by the United States. The commitment of American troops deepened over the years, as successive administrations grappled with the challenge of containing communism while avoiding direct confrontation with the Soviet Union.

Exploring the Impact: The Echoes of War in American Society

While the Vietnam War officially ended in 1975 with the fall of Saigon and the reunification of Vietnam under communist rule, its impact continues to reverberate through American society and culture to this day. The conflict left a profound legacy of division, disillusionment, and introspection, challenging long-held beliefs about American exceptionalism and the righteousness of military intervention.

One of the defining features of the Vietnam War was its polarizing effect on American society. As the conflict escalated, it sparked fierce debate and dissent, pitting proponents of military intervention against anti-war activists. The war at home was characterized by mass protests, draft resistance, and a burgeoning counterculture that rejected mainstream values and embraced alternative forms of expression.

The media played a pivotal role in shaping public perceptions of the war, bringing the grim realities of combat into American living rooms through vivid images and firsthand accounts. From the publication of the Pentagon Papers to the broadcast of the My Lai massacre, journalists exposed the contradictions and atrocities of the war, eroding public support and fueling anti-war sentiment.

At the same time, the Vietnam War served as a catalyst for profound social and cultural change in America. It gave rise to a generation of activists who challenged entrenched power structures and advocated for civil rights, women's liberation, and environmental protection. The war's impact was felt across all facets of American life, from literature and music to film and fashion, shaping the cultural landscape for years to come.

Outline of Subsequent Chapters: Navigating the Landscape of Echoes

In the pages that follow, we will embark on a journey through the echoes of the Vietnam War, exploring its lasting impact on American society and culture. Each chapter will delve into different aspects of the conflict and its aftermath, shedding light on the complexities of war, memory, and reconciliation in 20th-century America.

Chapter 2: Roots of Conflict - This chapter will examine the historical origins of the Vietnam War, from colonialism and nationalism to Cold War geopolitics, tracing the trajectory of American involvement in Southeast Asia.

Chapter 3: The War at Home - Here, we will explore the domestic repercussions of the Vietnam War, from the rise of the anti-war movement to the cultural transformations that swept through American society during the tumultuous 1960s and 70s.

Chapter 4: Soldiers' Stories - Through the firsthand accounts of Vietnam veterans, this chapter will offer insight into the experiences of those who served on the front lines, grappling with the physical and psychological toll of war.

Chapter 5: Consequences of Conflict - From the human cost of the war to its environmental and economic ramifications, this chapter will examine the enduring legacies of the Vietnam War for both Vietnam and the United States.

Chapter 6: Healing and Reconciliation - Here, we will explore the efforts to heal the wounds of war and foster reconciliation between former adversaries, reflecting on the importance of empathy and understanding in the pursuit of peace.

Chapter 7: Legacies and Lessons - This chapter will reflect on the enduring legacies of the Vietnam War and the lessons it holds for contemporary challenges and conflicts, offering insights into the complexities of war and memory.

As we embark on this journey through the echoes of the Vietnam War, we are reminded of the power of history to illuminate the present and guide us toward a more just and peaceful future. Through the stories of those who lived through this turbulent period, we gain a deeper understanding of the human cost of war and the resilience of the human spirit in the face of adversity.

Chapter 2: Roots of Conflict

Historical Context: Colonialism, Nationalism, and Cold War Dynamics

To understand the roots of the Vietnam War, one must delve into the complex historical context of colonialism, nationalism, and Cold War dynamics that shaped Southeast Asia in the 20th century. The seeds of conflict were sown long before the direct involvement of the United States, rooted in centuries of foreign intervention and indigenous resistance.

Colonialism in Vietnam traces back to the 19th century, when France established control over the region, known then as French Indochina. Exploiting Vietnam's resources and labor, the French imposed their authority through a system of indirect rule, exacerbating social and economic inequalities and fueling resentment among the Vietnamese population.

Nationalism emerged as a potent force in Vietnam in the early 20th century, driven by figures such as Ho Chi Minh, who sought to liberate the country from foreign domination and establish an independent state. Inspired by the principles of Marxism-Leninism and inspired by the success of anti-colonial movements elsewhere, Ho Chi Minh and his followers formed the Viet Minh, a revolutionary nationalist organization dedicated to overthrowing French rule.

The outbreak of World War II and the defeat of France by Nazi Germany provided an opportunity for the Viet Minh to escalate their resistance against the colonial regime. With Japanese occupation forces in control of Vietnam, Ho Chi Minh and his allies waged a guerrilla campaign against both the Japanese and the French, positioning themselves as the vanguard of Vietnamese liberation.

The end of World War II brought about a power vacuum in Indochina, as the collapse of colonial empires and the onset of the Cold

War created new opportunities and challenges for nationalist movements around the world. In Vietnam, the struggle for independence was caught in the crossfire of superpower rivalries, as the United States and the Soviet Union vied for influence in Southeast Asia.

The Domino Theory: Fear of Communism and American Involvement

Central to American involvement in Vietnam was the fear of communism spreading throughout Southeast Asia, a fear encapsulated by the Domino Theory. Coined by President Dwight D. Eisenhower in the 1950s, the Domino Theory posited that the fall of one country to communism would lead to a chain reaction of communist revolutions in neighboring countries, like a row of dominos falling one after another.

The Domino Theory reflected a deeply-held belief among American policymakers that the spread of communism posed an existential threat to global security and democracy. In the context of the Cold War, Vietnam was seen as a crucial battleground in the struggle against communist expansionism, with the potential to tip the balance of power in Asia and beyond.

The fear of communism was compounded by the geopolitical dynamics of the Cold War, as the United States sought to contain Soviet influence and prevent the spread of communism in strategically important regions. Vietnam, with its strategic location and rich natural resources, became a focal point of American efforts to counter communist influence and uphold the principles of containment.

Initial American Presence: From Advisors to Combat Troops

American involvement in Vietnam began in the early 1950s, initially in the form of military advisors sent to assist the French colonial forces in their struggle against the Viet Minh. Despite their efforts, the French suffered a humiliating defeat at the Battle of Dien Bien Phu in 1954, leading to the signing of the Geneva Accords and the division of Vietnam into North and South.

With the partition of Vietnam, the United States shifted its support to the anti-communist government of South Vietnam, led by Ngo Dinh Diem. Diem's authoritarian regime, marked by corruption and repression, struggled to maintain control in the face of growing opposition from communist insurgents and disaffected elements within the population.

As the situation in South Vietnam deteriorated, the Kennedy administration increased American military aid and advisors, hoping to bolster the regime and stem the tide of communist insurgency. However, the assassination of President Kennedy in 1963 and the subsequent escalation of the conflict under President Lyndon B. Johnson would see American involvement in Vietnam reach new heights.

The Gulf of Tonkin incident in August 1964 provided the pretext for direct American intervention, as Congress passed the Gulf of Tonkin Resolution authorizing the president to take all necessary measures to repel attacks against U.S. forces and prevent further aggression in Southeast Asia. This marked the beginning of a massive escalation of American military presence in Vietnam, as combat troops were deployed in increasing numbers to wage a protracted and ultimately futile war against the Viet Cong and North Vietnamese forces.

Escalation and Entrenchment: From Conflict to Quagmire

The escalation of American involvement in Vietnam marked a turning point in the conflict, as what began as a limited advisory mission evolved into a full-scale war of attrition. Despite the overwhelming superiority of American firepower, the communist forces proved resilient and resourceful, exploiting the rugged terrain and the support of local populations to wage a protracted guerrilla campaign.

The tactics employed by both sides reflected the brutal and indiscriminate nature of modern warfare, as villages were destroyed, civilians displaced, and atrocities committed on all sides. The use of chemical defoliants such as Agent Orange and the bombing of civilian targets raised moral and ethical questions about the conduct of the war and the treatment of non-combatants.

As the war dragged on, public support for the conflict waned, fueled by mounting casualties, economic strain, and growing disillusionment with the government's handling of the war. The anti-war movement, fueled by students, intellectuals, and grassroots activists, gained momentum, culminating in mass protests, draft resistance, and acts of civil disobedience that rocked American society to its core.

By the late 1960s, the Vietnam War had become a quagmire, with no clear end in sight and no easy solutions to the complex political, military, and moral dilemmas it presented. The Tet Offensive of 1968, though militarily inconclusive, shattered the myth of American invincibility and exposed the reality of a stalemated conflict with no clear path to victory.

The Roots of Conflict: Lessons from History

The Vietnam War was not merely a clash of arms, but a clash of ideologies, interests, and aspirations that reflected the broader currents of 20th-century history. It was a war of national liberation, a war of ideology, and a war of attrition, fueled by the competing visions of nationalism, communism, and anti-colonialism that shaped the post-war world.

The legacy of the Vietnam War continues to reverberate through American society and culture, reminding us of the enduring consequences of war and the complexities of power, ideology, and memory. It serves as a cautionary tale about the dangers of interventionism, the limits of military power, and the importance of understanding the historical context in which conflicts arise.

As we navigate the landscape of echoes left by the Vietnam War, we are confronted with difficult questions about the nature of power, the pursuit of justice, and the quest for peace in a world marked by conflict and uncertainty. By grappling with the roots of conflict in Vietnam, we gain insights into the forces that shape our world and the choices we make as individuals and as nations.

Chapter 3: The War at Home

Divided Nation: Societal Divisions and Dissent

The Vietnam War tore at the fabric of American society, igniting fierce debates and sparking widespread dissent that reverberated through communities, campuses, and households across the nation. The conflict exposed deep divisions over questions of morality, patriotism, and the role of the United States in the world, fracturing the consensus that had defined American foreign policy since World War II.

Protests against the war began almost as soon as American involvement escalated in the early 1960s, but it was not until the mid-to-late 1960s that the anti-war movement gained significant traction. Students, intellectuals, and activists mobilized in opposition to the war, organizing marches, rallies, and teach-ins to raise awareness and build solidarity. The movement transcended traditional political boundaries, drawing support from a broad spectrum of society, including religious leaders, labor unions, and veterans' organizations.

One of the most prominent forms of dissent was draft resistance, as young men across the country refused to comply with conscription orders and risked imprisonment to protest the war. Some sought conscientious objector status, citing moral or religious objections to military service, while others went underground or fled the country to avoid the draft altogether. The draft became a lightning rod for opposition to the war, symbolizing the injustice and inequality of a conflict in which the burden of service fell disproportionately on the poor and marginalized.

The war also gave rise to a vibrant counterculture movement that rejected mainstream values and embraced alternative lifestyles, artistic expression, and political activism. From the hippie communes of Haight-Ashbury to the music festivals of Woodstock, the counterculture provided a space for dissent and experimentation, challenging conventional norms and celebrating the ideals of peace, love, and freedom. Rock music became a powerful medium for social critique, with artists such as Bob Dylan, Joan Baez, and Creedence Clearwater Revival penning anthems of protest and resistance that captured the spirit of the times.

Media's Role: Shaping Perceptions and Shifting Paradigms

The Vietnam War was the first televised war, bringing the grim realities of combat into American living rooms through vivid images and firsthand accounts. From the nightly news broadcasts of CBS, NBC, and ABC to the photojournalism of magazines like Life and Time, the media played a pivotal role in shaping public perceptions of the war and influencing government policy.

Television coverage of the war brought the horrors of combat into American homes in a way that had never been seen before. Viewers watched in horror as images of wounded soldiers, burning villages, and napalm strikes filled their screens, challenging the sanitized narratives of heroism and victory propagated by government officials and military leaders. The juxtaposition of images of war with scenes of everyday life back home forced viewers to confront the human cost of the conflict and raised troubling questions about its justification and morality.

The media's coverage of the war also played a key role in shaping public opinion and influencing government policy. Journalists such as David Halberstam, Neil Sheehan, and Seymour Hersh exposed the contradictions and atrocities of the war, from the My Lai massacre to the secret bombing campaigns in Laos and Cambodia. Their reporting eroded public support for the war and fueled anti-war sentiment, contributing to a climate of skepticism and distrust that permeated American society.

The cultural impact of the war extended beyond journalism to literature, music, and film, as artists and writers grappled with the moral and existential questions raised by the conflict. Novels such as Tim O'Brien's "The Things They Carried" and Michael Herr's "Dispatches" offered searing accounts of the war's human toll, while films like "Apocalypse Now" and "Platoon" depicted the madness and futility of combat in Vietnam. In music, artists such as John Lennon, Marvin Gaye, and Country Joe McDonald used their platforms to voice opposition to the war and express solidarity with those who resisted it.

Cultural Impact: Literature, Music, and Film as Vehicles for Protest and Reflection

The Vietnam War had a profound impact on American culture, influencing literature, music, and film in ways that continue to resonate to this day. The war served as a backdrop for some of the most enduring works of art and literature of the 20th century, offering a lens through which to explore themes of trauma, memory, and the human condition.

In literature, the Vietnam War inspired a new wave of writing that sought to capture the visceral experience of combat and the moral ambiguities of war. Writers such as Tim O'Brien, Philip Caputo, and Larry Heinemann drew on their own experiences as soldiers to create works of fiction that blurred the line between fact and fiction, reality and imagination. Their novels explored the psychological toll of war, the bonds of brotherhood forged in battle, and the struggle to make sense of a senseless conflict.

Music also played a central role in the anti-war movement, providing a soundtrack for protest and resistance that resonated with a generation of young Americans. Artists such as Bob Dylan, Joan Baez, and Phil Ochs penned songs of protest and solidarity that captured the spirit of the times, while bands like Creedence Clearwater Revival and Buffalo Springfield used their music to express outrage at the war and call for its end. The music of the era served as a rallying cry for a generation disillusioned with the status quo, offering solace and inspiration in the face of uncertainty and despair.

Film emerged as another powerful medium for exploring the impact of the Vietnam War on American society and culture. Directors such as Stanley Kubrick, Francis Ford Coppola, and Oliver Stone created cinematic masterpieces that depicted the madness and horror of war with unflinching honesty. Films like "Apocalypse Now," "The Deer Hunter," and "Platoon" offered audiences a visceral glimpse into the heart of darkness that lay at the heart of the Vietnam War, challenging viewers to confront uncomfortable truths about the nature of violence, power, and human nature.

In Conclusion: The War at Home and Its Lasting Legacy

The Vietnam War was more than a military conflict; it was a cultural and social phenomenon that reshaped American society and left an indelible mark on the nation's collective memory. The war exposed deep divisions within American society, pitting supporters of the war against opponents in a bitter struggle for the soul of the nation.

The media played a pivotal role in shaping public perceptions of the war and influencing government policy, bringing the realities of combat into American living rooms and challenging the sanitized narratives propagated by official sources. Literature, music, and film provided a means of expression for those who opposed the war, offering a platform for protest and reflection that resonated with millions of Americans.

The cultural impact of the Vietnam War continues to reverberate through American society and culture to this day, reminding us of the power of art and literature to bear witness to the human cost of war and to give voice to those who have been silenced by violence. As we grapple with the legacy of the Vietnam War, we are confronted with difficult questions about the nature of power, the pursuit of justice, and the quest for peace in a world marked by conflict and uncertainty. Through the stories of those who lived through this tumultuous period, we gain a deeper understanding of the enduring consequences of war and the resilience of the human spirit in the face of adversity.

Chapter 4: Soldiers' Stories

Personal Narratives: The Voices of Vietnam Veterans

The Vietnam War was fought not only on the battlefields of Southeast Asia but also in the hearts and minds of the soldiers who served there. For the men and women who answered the call of duty, the war was a deeply personal and transformative experience that left an indelible mark on their lives. Through their personal narratives, we gain insight into the human cost of war and the complexities of the Vietnam War experience.

For many Vietnam veterans, the war began as a distant and abstract concept, a far-off conflict in a foreign land that seemed disconnected from their everyday lives. But as they arrived in Vietnam and found themselves thrust into the chaos and confusion of combat, the reality of war became all too real. From the jungles of the Mekong Delta to the highlands of the Central Highlands, soldiers faced a relentless barrage of enemy fire, ambushes, and booby traps that tested their courage and resilience in ways they could never have imagined.

The bonds forged in the crucible of combat were unlike any other, as soldiers relied on one another for survival and support in the face of overwhelming adversity. From the camaraderie of the battlefield to the quiet moments of reflection in the trenches, the shared experiences of war created a bond that transcended race, class, and background, uniting soldiers in a common struggle for survival and meaning.

But for many Vietnam veterans, the war did not end when they returned home. The memories of combat lingered long after the last shots had been fired, haunting their dreams and shaping their perceptions of the world around them. The transition from the battlefield to civilian life was often fraught with challenges, as veterans struggled to make sense of their experiences and find their place in a society that seemed indifferent to their sacrifices.

Psychological Toll: The Hidden Wounds of War

The Vietnam War took a heavy toll on the mental health of those who served, leaving many veterans grappling with the invisible wounds of trauma and loss. Post-Traumatic Stress Disorder (PTSD), a condition characterized by flashbacks, nightmares, and hypervigilance, emerged as one of the defining legacies of the war, affecting an estimated 30% of Vietnam veterans.

For veterans with PTSD, the war never truly ends, as the memories of combat continue to intrude into their daily lives, triggering intense emotional reactions and feelings of guilt, shame, and anger. Many veterans turned to self-medication as a way of coping with their symptoms, leading to high rates of substance abuse, homelessness, and suicide among Vietnam veterans.

The stigma surrounding mental illness made it difficult for veterans to seek help for their PTSD, as they feared being labeled as weak or unstable by their peers and superiors. As a result, many suffered in silence, enduring years of pain and suffering without access to the care and support they so desperately needed.

It was not until decades later that the true extent of the psychological toll of the Vietnam War began to be recognized, as veterans and their families began to speak out about their experiences and advocate for greater awareness and understanding of PTSD. Today, thanks to the efforts of grassroots organizations and advocacy groups, Vietnam veterans have access to a wide range of mental health services and support networks to help them cope with the lasting effects of their wartime experiences.

Legacy of Service: Honoring the Sacrifice of Vietnam Veterans

Despite the challenges they faced, Vietnam veterans have made significant contributions to American society in the decades since the war ended. From advocacy and activism to entrepreneurship and public service, Vietnam veterans have played a vital role in shaping the course of American history and ensuring that the sacrifices of their comrades will never be forgotten.

Many Vietnam veterans have become leading voices in the fight for veterans' rights and benefits, advocating for improved healthcare, disability compensation, and recognition for the contributions of all who served. Organizations such as the Vietnam Veterans of America (VVA) and the Disabled American Veterans (DAV) have played a central role in this effort, providing support and resources to veterans and their families across the country.

In addition to their advocacy work, Vietnam veterans have also made significant contributions to American culture and society through their artistic and entrepreneurial endeavors. From bestselling novels and award-winning films to successful businesses and nonprofit organizations, Vietnam veterans have used their talents and skills to make a positive impact on the world around them, inspiring future generations to learn from the lessons of the past and strive for a better future.

The legacy of Vietnam veterans serves as a reminder of the enduring spirit of service and sacrifice that defines the American experience. Despite the challenges they faced and the wounds they carry, Vietnam veterans have remained steadfast in their commitment to their fellow veterans and their country, embodying the values of courage, resilience, and patriotism that have always defined the American spirit. As we honor their sacrifices and celebrate their achievements, we must also recommit ourselves to ensuring that all veterans receive the care, support, and recognition they deserve for their service to our nation.

Chapter 5: Consequences of Conflict

The Vietnam War exacted a heavy toll on both human lives and the environment, leaving behind a legacy of suffering, destruction, and long-term consequences that continue to shape the lives of millions of people in Vietnam and the United States. In this chapter, we will examine the multifaceted impacts of the war, from the staggering human cost to the environmental and economic ramifications that persist to this day.

Human Cost: The Toll of War

The human cost of the Vietnam War was staggering, with millions of lives lost and countless more shattered by the violence and trauma of conflict. According to estimates, between 2 to 3 million Vietnamese civilians and soldiers were killed during the war, along with over 58,000 American service members and hundreds of thousands of soldiers from other countries involved in the conflict.

The war's toll on civilian populations was particularly devastating, as indiscriminate bombings, artillery shelling, and ground combat exacted a heavy toll on innocent men, women, and children caught in the crossfire. Entire villages were destroyed, crops were burned, and livelihoods were shattered, leaving behind a landscape scarred by the ravages of war.

For the soldiers who served in Vietnam, the toll of war extended far beyond the battlefield, as many returned home with physical injuries, psychological scars, and emotional wounds that would never fully heal. The prevalence of post-traumatic stress disorder (PTSD) among Vietnam veterans remains high, with studies estimating that as many as 30% of veterans suffer from the condition, leading to high rates of substance abuse, homelessness, and suicide.

The impact of the war on families and communities was profound, as thousands of children were orphaned, families were torn apart, and communities were left to grapple with the loss of loved ones and the trauma of war. The wounds of the Vietnam War continue to reverberate through generations, as descendants of veterans and survivors struggle to come to terms with the legacy of the conflict and its enduring consequences.

Environmental Impact: Ecological Devastation and Agent Orange

The environmental impact of the Vietnam War was widespread and devastating, as decades of chemical warfare and defoliation efforts left behind a toxic legacy that continues to haunt the Vietnamese landscape to this day. One of the most notorious examples of environmental destruction during the war was the widespread use of Agent Orange, a toxic herbicide sprayed by American forces to destroy vegetation and deny cover to enemy forces.

Despite its intended purpose, Agent Orange had far-reaching and devastating consequences for both human health and the environment, contaminating soil, water, and air with dioxin, a highly toxic chemical compound linked to a range of health problems, including cancer, birth defects, and neurological disorders. Millions of Vietnamese civilians and soldiers were exposed to Agent Orange during the war, leading to widespread suffering and long-term health consequences that continue to affect generations of Vietnamese people.

The ecological devastation caused by Agent Orange and other chemical defoliants was catastrophic, destroying vast swathes of forest, contaminating water sources, and disrupting fragile ecosystems that were home to countless species of plants and animals. In addition to its direct impact on the environment, Agent Orange also had indirect consequences, as the loss of vegetation and disruption of ecosystems contributed to soil erosion, loss of biodiversity, and long-term degradation of land and water resources.

Despite efforts to clean up contaminated sites and provide assistance to affected communities, the environmental legacy of the Vietnam War remains a pressing concern, as dioxin contamination continues to pose a threat to human health and the environment. The ongoing efforts of governments, NGOs, and international organizations to address the environmental legacy of the war are essential to mitigating its long-term impacts and ensuring a sustainable future for Vietnam and its people.

Economic Ramifications: Long-Term Costs and Challenges

The economic ramifications of the Vietnam War were profound, affecting both Vietnam and the United States in ways that continue to shape their economies and societies to this day. For Vietnam, the war exacted a heavy toll on the country's infrastructure, economy, and social fabric, leaving behind a legacy of poverty, underdevelopment, and economic dependency that persists to this day.

The cost of the war in human lives and resources was immense, diverting precious resources away from social and economic development and leaving the country ill-equipped to address the pressing needs of its population. In the aftermath of the war, Vietnam faced daunting challenges, including widespread poverty, food shortages, and a lack of basic infrastructure, as well as the task of rebuilding a country shattered by decades of conflict.

The economic impact of the war was also felt in the United States, as the cost of financing the war strained the country's economy and contributed to rising inflation, unemployment, and social unrest. The war's impact on the U.S. economy was compounded by the loss of American lives and the long-term costs of caring for veterans and their families, as well as the economic consequences of the war's broader geopolitical implications.

In addition to its immediate economic costs, the Vietnam War also had long-term consequences for both Vietnam and the United States, shaping the trajectory of their economies and societies for decades to come. In Vietnam, the war left behind a legacy of economic dependency and underdevelopment that continues to hinder the country's efforts to achieve sustainable growth and prosperity. In the United States, the war's economic legacy is evident in the ongoing challenges of caring for veterans, addressing the social and economic disparities that persist in communities affected by the war, and reconciling the costs of war with the country's broader economic priorities.

In Conclusion: Grappling with the Consequences of Conflict

The consequences of the Vietnam War are far-reaching and enduring, shaping the lives of millions of people in Vietnam and the United States and leaving behind a legacy of suffering, destruction, and resilience. From the staggering human cost of war to the environmental and economic ramifications that persist to this day, the Vietnam War continues to serve as a sobering reminder of the true cost of conflict and the urgent need for peace, reconciliation, and sustainable development in a world marked by violence and uncertainty. As we grapple with the consequences of the Vietnam War, we are reminded of the importance of learning from the mistakes of the past and working together to build a better future for generations to come.

Chapter 6: Healing and Reconciliation

In the aftermath of the Vietnam War, a shattered landscape of broken lives, divided nations, and lingering trauma awaited those who sought to pick up the pieces and move forward. Healing and reconciliation became imperative for both Vietnam and the United States, as they grappled with the scars of war and sought to forge a path toward peace and understanding. In this chapter, we will explore the efforts aimed at healing the wounds of war, promoting reconciliation, and fostering a sense of closure for those affected by the conflict.

Post-War Reconciliation Efforts: Bridges Across Divides

Despite the bitterness and animosity that marked the war, efforts to promote reconciliation between Vietnam and the United States began almost immediately after the guns fell silent. Diplomatic exchanges, cultural exchanges, and people-to-people initiatives sought to bridge the gap between former enemies and promote understanding and cooperation in the aftermath of the conflict.

One of the most visible symbols of reconciliation between Vietnam and the United States is the normalization of diplomatic relations in 1995, which paved the way for a new era of engagement and cooperation between the two countries. Since then, the relationship between Vietnam and the United States has grown significantly, with increased trade, investment, and cultural exchange strengthening ties between the two nations and fostering mutual understanding and respect.

Memorialization also played a crucial role in the process of reconciliation, as both Vietnam and the United States sought to honor the memory of those who lost their lives in the war and acknowledge the sacrifices made by veterans and their families. Memorials, museums, and commemorative events served as reminders of the human cost of war and the importance of remembering the past in order to build a better future.

One of the most poignant examples of memorialization is the Vietnam Veterans Memorial in Washington, D.C., which serves as a powerful tribute to the more than 58,000 American service members who died in the war. Designed by Maya Lin and dedicated in 1982, the memorial's stark black granite walls bear the names of those who made the ultimate sacrifice, providing a place of solace and remembrance for veterans and their families.

Veterans' Advocacy: Support and Solidarity

Vietnam veterans played a central role in the efforts to promote healing and reconciliation in the aftermath of the war, advocating for recognition, support, and understanding for those who served and sacrificed in Vietnam. Organizations such as the Vietnam Veterans of America (VVA), the Disabled American Veterans (DAV), and the Vietnam Veterans Memorial Fund (VVMF) have been at the forefront of these efforts, providing support and resources to veterans and their families across the country.

Through their advocacy work, Vietnam veterans have sought to raise awareness about the challenges facing those who served in Vietnam, including the prevalence of PTSD, the long-term health effects of exposure to Agent Orange, and the difficulties of reintegrating into civilian life after the trauma of war. They have also been vocal advocates for peace and reconciliation, speaking out against the glorification of war and the perpetuation of violence in all its forms.

One of the most significant contributions of Vietnam veterans to the cause of healing and reconciliation has been their commitment to supporting their Vietnamese counterparts and promoting friendship and understanding between the two nations. Through initiatives such as the Vietnam Veterans of America Foundation's humanitarian projects and the Veterans for Peace's reconciliation tours, veterans have worked to build bridges of friendship and cooperation between Vietnam and the United States, fostering a spirit of solidarity and mutual respect that transcends borders and divisions.

Lessons Learned: Toward a More Peaceful Future

The Vietnam War was a painful and divisive chapter in the history of both Vietnam and the United States, but it also provided valuable lessons about the true cost of war and the importance of reconciliation in preventing future conflicts. As we reflect on the legacy of the war, we are reminded of the need to confront the past, acknowledge the wounds of war, and work together to build a more peaceful and just world for future generations.

One of the most important lessons of the Vietnam War is the power of reconciliation to heal the wounds of conflict and promote understanding and cooperation between former adversaries. By acknowledging the pain and suffering caused by war and working together to address the root causes of violence and injustice, we can build a more inclusive and compassionate society that values peace, justice, and human dignity above all else.

The efforts to promote healing and reconciliation in the aftermath of the Vietnam War remind us that the path to peace is not easy or straightforward, but it is worth pursuing with determination and humility. Through dialogue, empathy, and mutual respect, we can overcome the divisions that divide us and build a world where conflict is resolved through diplomacy and dialogue, rather than violence and coercion.

In Conclusion: Building a Better Future

The Vietnam War was a tragedy that left deep scars on both Vietnam and the United States, but it also provided an opportunity for healing, reconciliation, and growth. As we look to the future, let us remember the lessons of the past and work together to build a more peaceful and just world for future generations. By embracing the values of compassion, solidarity, and mutual respect, we can honor the sacrifices of those who came before us and create a legacy of peace and reconciliation that will endure for generations to come.

Chapter 7: Legacies and Lessons

The Vietnam War holds a unique place in American history, its legacy shaping not only the lives of those who lived through it but also the trajectory of the nation itself. In this chapter, we will delve into the enduring legacies of the Vietnam War, the lessons that can be drawn from its tumultuous history, and the significance of memorialization in preserving the memory of those who served and sacrificed.

Enduring Legacies: Shaping American Foreign Policy and National Identity

The Vietnam War cast a long shadow over American foreign policy, military doctrine, and national identity, leaving behind a legacy that continues to shape the nation's approach to war, diplomacy, and international relations. From the halls of power in Washington to the streets of small towns across America, the Vietnam War remains a defining chapter in the nation's history, its lessons and legacies reverberating through the corridors of power and the collective consciousness of the American people.

One of the most enduring legacies of the Vietnam War is its impact on American foreign policy, as policymakers grappled with the lessons learned from the conflict and sought to avoid the mistakes of the past in future military interventions. The war's quagmire, marked by escalation, stalemate, and eventual withdrawal, reinforced the dangers of interventionism and the limits of military power, leading to a more cautious and restrained approach to foreign policy in the post-Vietnam era.

The Vietnam War also left a lasting imprint on American military doctrine, as the lessons learned from the conflict reshaped the way the U.S. military approached warfare and counterinsurgency operations. The emphasis on counterinsurgency, irregular warfare, and hearts and minds campaigns became central tenets of military strategy in the post-Vietnam era, as the military sought to adapt to the changing nature of conflict in the modern world.

In addition to its impact on foreign policy and military doctrine, the Vietnam War also left an indelible mark on the national identity of the United States, shaping the way Americans view themselves and their place in the world. The war's divisive and contentious nature, marked by protests, dissent, and disillusionment, challenged traditional notions of patriotism and national unity, forcing Americans to confront uncomfortable truths about the nature of power, politics, and the human cost of war.

Learning from History: Drawing Lessons for Contemporary Conflicts

The Vietnam War offers valuable lessons for contemporary conflicts and international relations, providing insights into the complexities of war, diplomacy, and the human condition. By examining the mistakes and missteps of the past, we can gain a deeper understanding of the challenges and opportunities facing us in the present and chart a course toward a more peaceful and just future.

One of the most important lessons of the Vietnam War is the importance of understanding the historical, political, and cultural context in which conflicts arise. By recognizing the complex web of factors that contribute to the outbreak of war, we can better anticipate the consequences of our actions and avoid the pitfalls of interventionism and militarism.

Another key lesson of the Vietnam War is the importance of diplomacy and dialogue in resolving conflicts and promoting peace. Despite the bitter and protracted nature of the war, diplomatic efforts ultimately played a crucial role in ending the conflict and laying the groundwork for reconciliation between former adversaries. By prioritizing diplomacy over military force, we can avoid the human suffering and devastation that often accompany armed conflict and build a more peaceful and stable world for future generations.

Memorialization: Preserving the Memory of War

Memorialization plays a crucial role in preserving the memory of the Vietnam War and honoring the sacrifices of those who served and sacrificed in the conflict. Memorials, museums, and commemorative events serve as reminders of the human cost of war and provide a space for reflection, remembrance, and reconciliation for veterans, their families, and the broader community.

One of the most iconic memorials dedicated to the Vietnam War is the Vietnam Veterans Memorial in Washington, D.C., which serves as a powerful tribute to the more than 58,000 American service members who died in the conflict. Designed by Maya Lin and dedicated in 1982, the memorial's stark black granite walls bear the names of those who made the ultimate sacrifice, providing a place of solace and remembrance for veterans and their families.

In addition to physical memorials, the Vietnam War is also commemorated through a variety of cultural and educational initiatives, including documentaries, films, books, and oral history projects that seek to preserve the stories and experiences of those who lived through the war. These efforts help ensure that the memory of the Vietnam War lives on for future generations, serving as a reminder of the human cost of war and the importance of working together to build a more peaceful and just world.

In Conclusion: Honoring the Past, Building the Future

The Vietnam War continues to shape the lives of millions of people in Vietnam and the United States, its legacies and lessons serving as reminders of the enduring consequences of conflict and the importance of reconciliation in building a more peaceful and just world. As we honor the sacrifices of those who served and sacrificed in the war, let us also recommit ourselves to the values of peace, justice, and human dignity that they fought to uphold. By learning from the mistakes of the past and working together to build a better future, we can ensure that the memory of the Vietnam War lives on as a testament to the resilience of the human spirit and the power of hope in the face of adversity.

Chapter 8: The Vietnam Syndrome

The Vietnam War left an indelible mark on American society and politics, shaping public attitudes toward war, military intervention, and presidential power in profound and lasting ways. In the aftermath of the conflict, the United States grappled with the legacy of Vietnam, confronting the enduring impact of what came to be known as the "Vietnam Syndrome." In this chapter, we will explore the origins of the Vietnam Syndrome, its implications for American foreign policy and military strategy, and its ongoing relevance in contemporary debates about war and presidential power.

The "Vietnam Syndrome": A Crisis of Confidence

The term "Vietnam Syndrome" was coined in the aftermath of the Vietnam War to describe the collective trauma and disillusionment that gripped American society in its wake. Characterized by a deep-seated skepticism of military interventionism and a reluctance to engage in foreign conflicts, the Vietnam Syndrome represented a fundamental shift in public attitudes toward war and the use of military force.

At its core, the Vietnam Syndrome reflected a crisis of confidence in American leadership and institutions, as the nation grappled with the moral, political, and psychological wounds inflicted by the war. The staggering human cost of Vietnam, coupled with the failure to achieve victory or establish a stable government in South Vietnam, led many Americans to question the wisdom of military intervention and the efficacy of U.S. foreign policy.

The Vietnam Syndrome also had profound implications for American military interventions in the years following the war, as policymakers sought to avoid the mistakes and missteps of Vietnam and restore public trust in the government's ability to conduct foreign policy.

The legacy of Vietnam loomed large over subsequent conflicts, from the Persian Gulf War to the wars in Iraq and Afghanistan, shaping the way policymakers approached questions of war and peace and influencing public attitudes toward military intervention.

War Powers Debate: Constitutional Questions and Presidential Authority

One of the central issues raised by the Vietnam War was the question of presidential war powers and the balance of power between the executive and legislative branches of government. The Vietnam War saw the erosion of congressional authority over war-making powers, as successive administrations expanded the scope of executive authority to conduct military operations without congressional approval.

The Gulf of Tonkin Resolution, passed by Congress in 1964, provided President Lyndon B. Johnson with broad authority to escalate U.S. military involvement in Vietnam without a formal declaration of war. This marked a significant departure from the constitutional framework established by the Founding Fathers, which vested the power to declare war in the hands of Congress, not the president.

The war powers debate sparked by Vietnam raised important constitutional questions about the limits of presidential authority and the role of Congress in matters of war and peace. Critics argued that the executive branch had exceeded its constitutional authority by waging war without congressional approval, while defenders of executive power contended that the president had inherent authority as commander-in-chief to respond to threats to national security.

In the years following Vietnam, Congress sought to reassert its authority over war powers through a series of legislative measures, including the War Powers Resolution of 1973, which sought to limit the president's ability to deploy U.S. armed forces without congressional authorization. Despite these efforts, the balance of power between the executive and legislative branches remains a subject of debate and contention to this day, as presidents continue to assert broad authority to conduct military operations without congressional approval.

Reevaluation of Military Strategy: Lessons Learned from Vietnam

The Vietnam War also prompted a reevaluation of American military strategy and doctrine, as policymakers sought to learn from the mistakes and missteps of the conflict and adapt to the changing nature of warfare in the modern world. The lessons of Vietnam influenced subsequent military thinking and strategic planning, shaping the way the U.S. military approached questions of strategy, tactics, and force projection in the post-Vietnam era.

One of the most important lessons of Vietnam was the need for flexibility and adaptability in military planning and execution. The Vietnam War exposed the limitations of conventional military tactics in unconventional warfare environments, as American forces struggled to counter the guerrilla tactics and asymmetric warfare tactics employed by the Viet Cong and North Vietnamese Army.

In response to the lessons of Vietnam, the U.S. military adopted a more flexible and nuanced approach to warfare, emphasizing the importance of counterinsurgency, irregular warfare, and population-centric strategies in combating insurgent groups and non-state actors. The development of new doctrine and tactics, such as the Army's Field Manual 3-24 on Counterinsurgency Operations and the Marine Corps' Small Wars Manual, reflected a broader shift in military thinking toward a more holistic and multidimensional approach to conflict.

The Vietnam War also prompted a reassessment of the role of air power in modern warfare, as policymakers grappled with the limitations and effectiveness of strategic bombing campaigns in achieving political and military objectives. The failure of the bombing campaigns in Vietnam to break the will of the enemy or force a negotiated settlement led to a reevaluation of the utility of air power as a strategic tool of coercion, prompting a renewed emphasis on precision-guided munitions and targeted strikes in future military operations.

In Conclusion: The Vietnam Syndrome and Its Legacy

The Vietnam War left an indelible mark on American society and politics, its legacy shaping public attitudes toward war, presidential power, and military strategy for decades to come. The Vietnam Syndrome represented a crisis of confidence in American leadership and institutions, as the nation grappled with the moral, political, and psychological wounds inflicted by the war.

The war powers debate sparked by Vietnam raised important constitutional questions about the limits of presidential authority and the role of Congress in matters of war and peace, while the reevaluation of military strategy prompted a shift in thinking toward a more flexible and nuanced approach to conflict.

As we reflect on the legacy of Vietnam, we are reminded of the enduring consequences of war and the importance of learning from the mistakes of the past. By confronting the lessons of Vietnam with humility and honesty, we can build a more peaceful and just world for future generations, one that values diplomacy, dialogue, and cooperation over violence and coercion.

Chapter 9: Cultural Representations

The Vietnam War occupies a unique place in American cultural memory, its impact extending far beyond the battlefield to shape the way we understand and interpret the complexities of war, trauma, and memory. In this chapter, we will explore the multifaceted cultural representations of the Vietnam War, from literature and film to television and art, examining the ways in which these representations have shaped public perception and memory of the war and its legacy.

Vietnam in Popular Culture: A Multifaceted Tapestry

The Vietnam War has been a subject of fascination and fascination in popular culture for decades, inspiring a rich and diverse array of artistic interpretations that reflect the complexities and contradictions of the conflict. From bestselling novels and award-winning films to hit television series and groundbreaking works of art, Vietnam has loomed large in the cultural imagination, providing a lens through which we can explore the human cost of war and the enduring legacy of trauma.

One of the most enduring and influential cultural representations of the Vietnam War is literature, with countless novels, short stories, and memoirs offering powerful and often haunting insights into the experiences of soldiers, veterans, and civilians caught up in the maelstrom of war. Works such as Tim O'Brien's "The Things They Carried," Philip Caputo's "A Rumor of War," and Michael Herr's "Dispatches" have become canonical texts in the literature of war, capturing the raw intensity and emotional complexity of the Vietnam experience with unflinching honesty and compassion.

In addition to literature, the Vietnam War has also been a fertile subject for filmmakers, with directors such as Oliver Stone, Francis Ford Coppola, and Stanley Kubrick producing some of the most iconic and influential films in cinematic history. From Stone's searing indictment of the war in "Platoon" to Coppola's hallucinatory epic "Apocalypse Now" and Kubrick's darkly satirical "Full Metal Jacket," these films have shaped public perception of the war and its legacy, offering a visceral and immersive glimpse into the horrors and absurdities of combat.

Television has also played a significant role in shaping cultural representations of the Vietnam War, with landmark series such as Ken Burns and Lynn Novick's "The Vietnam War" and Tom Hanks and Steven Spielberg's "Band of Brothers" providing nuanced and in-depth explorations of the conflict and its impact on those who served. Through archival footage, interviews with veterans, and expert analysis, these programs have offered viewers a comprehensive and compelling portrait of the war and its enduring legacy.

Art has also been a powerful medium for exploring the Vietnam War and its legacy, with artists such as Robert Rauschenberg, Jasper Johns, and Leon Golub producing powerful and provocative works that confront the trauma and violence of war with unflinching honesty and courage. From Rauschenberg's iconic "Vietnam" series to Golub's harrowing depictions of torture and suffering, these artists have used their work to bear witness to the human cost of war and to challenge viewers to confront uncomfortable truths about violence, power, and memory.

Myth vs. Reality: Navigating the Complexities of Cultural Representation

While cultural representations of the Vietnam War have provided valuable insights into the human experience of conflict, they have also perpetuated myths and stereotypes that have shaped public perception and memory of the war in complex and often contradictory ways. From the romanticized heroism of Hollywood blockbusters to the gritty realism of documentary filmmaking, these representations have shaped the way we understand and interpret the complexities of war, trauma, and memory.

One of the most enduring myths of the Vietnam War is the image of the traumatized veteran, haunted by the horrors of combat and struggling to reintegrate into civilian life. While this image is grounded in truth, it has also served to oversimplify and stereotype the experiences of Vietnam veterans, reducing their stories to a single narrative of suffering and victimhood. In reality, Vietnam veterans are a diverse and complex group of individuals, each with their own unique experiences and perspectives on the war and its legacy.

Another common myth of the Vietnam War is the notion of American exceptionalism, the belief that the United States was uniquely qualified to intervene in Vietnam and impose its will on the Vietnamese people. This myth has been perpetuated by popular culture, which has often portrayed American soldiers as noble heroes fighting against an evil enemy, while downplaying or ignoring the complexities of the conflict and its root causes. In reality, the Vietnam War was a deeply flawed and morally ambiguous conflict, marked by widespread human rights abuses, atrocities, and systemic failures of leadership and policy.

The Evolution of Narratives: Tracing the Changing Portrayal of Vietnam Veterans and the War's Legacy

Over the decades since the end of the Vietnam War, cultural representations of Vietnam veterans and the war's legacy have evolved and shifted in response to changing social, political, and cultural dynamics. In the immediate aftermath of the war, Vietnam veterans were often portrayed as victims of a misguided and unjust war, struggling to cope with the physical and psychological wounds inflicted by combat and the indifference of a society that had turned its back on them.

In the 1980s and 1990s, however, a new generation of Vietnam veterans emerged, reclaiming their stories and challenging prevailing stereotypes and misconceptions about their service and sacrifice. Through organizations such as the Vietnam Veterans of America (VVA) and advocacy groups like the Vietnam Veterans Memorial Fund (VVMF), veterans began to speak out about their experiences and demand recognition and respect for their service.

This shift in narrative was reflected in popular culture, with films such as "Born on the Fourth of July" and "Coming Home" offering nuanced and empathetic portrayals of Vietnam veterans grappling with the trauma of war and the challenges of reintegration into civilian life. These films humanized veterans, depicting them as complex and multidimensional individuals with hopes, dreams, and struggles like anyone else.

In recent years, cultural representations of the Vietnam War and its legacy have continued to evolve, as younger generations of artists, filmmakers, and writers have sought to explore new perspectives and narratives on the conflict. From the perspectives of Vietnamese civilians and soldiers to the experiences of women and minorities in the war, these new voices have expanded the boundaries of our understanding of Vietnam and its enduring impact on American society and culture.

In Conclusion: The Power of Cultural Representation

Cultural representations of the Vietnam War have played a powerful and profound role in shaping public perception and memory of the conflict, providing a lens through which we can explore the human experience of war and its enduring legacy. From literature and film to television and art, these representations have offered insights into the complexities of trauma, memory, and resilience, challenging us to confront uncomfortable truths about the nature of violence, power, and memory.

As we continue to grapple with the legacy of the Vietnam War, it is important to recognize the power and potential of cultural representation to shape our understanding of the past and our vision for the future. By engaging with diverse and nuanced portrayals of Vietnam and its legacy, we can gain new insights into the human cost of war and the enduring resilience of the human spirit, inspiring us to work towards a more peaceful and just world for future generations.

Chapter 10: Vietnam War Tourism

Vietnam War tourism has emerged as a significant industry, drawing visitors from around the world to explore the sites and stories associated with one of the most consequential conflicts of the 20th century. In this chapter, we will delve into the phenomenon of Vietnam War tourism, examining its impact on local communities and historical memory, highlighting significant landmarks and memorials related to the conflict, and exploring the ethical considerations surrounding the commodification of war-related experiences for tourism purposes.

War Tourism Industry: Exploring the Phenomenon

War tourism, also known as dark tourism or thanatourism, refers to the practice of visiting sites associated with war, conflict, and tragedy for leisure, educational, or commemorative purposes. From the battlefields of World War I to the concentration camps of World War II, war tourism encompasses a wide range of sites and experiences that offer visitors a glimpse into the human cost of war and the enduring legacy of conflict.

In Vietnam, war tourism has become a significant industry, attracting millions of visitors each year to explore the country's rich and complex history, including its tumultuous experience during the Vietnam War. From the bustling streets of Hanoi to the lush landscapes of the Mekong Delta, Vietnam offers a wealth of opportunities for tourists to engage with the country's past and learn about the impact of the war on its people and culture.

One of the most popular destinations for war tourism in Vietnam is Ho Chi Minh City, formerly known as Saigon, which served as the capital of South Vietnam during the war. Visitors can explore historic sites such as the Reunification Palace, the War Remnants Museum, and the Cu Chi Tunnels, which offer insights into the experiences of both Vietnamese and American soldiers during the conflict.

In addition to Ho Chi Minh City, other popular destinations for war tourism in Vietnam include the former demilitarized zone (DMZ) along the border between North and South Vietnam, where visitors can explore historic sites such as the Vinh Moc Tunnels, the Khe Sanh Combat Base, and the Hien Luong Bridge, which served as a symbolic dividing line between North and South Vietnam during the war.

Commemorative Sites: Remembering the Past

Commemorative sites play a crucial role in preserving the memory of the Vietnam War and honoring the sacrifices of those who served and sacrificed in the conflict. From iconic landmarks in Vietnam to solemn memorials in the United States, these sites serve as reminders of the human cost of war and provide a space for reflection, remembrance, and reconciliation for veterans, their families, and the broader community.

In Vietnam, one of the most significant commemorative sites related to the Vietnam War is the War Remnants Museum in Ho Chi Minh City, which offers visitors a comprehensive overview of the conflict and its impact on Vietnamese society and culture. The museum's exhibits include photographs, artifacts, and multimedia displays that document the atrocities of war, including the effects of chemical weapons such as Agent Orange and the suffering of civilian populations caught in the crossfire.

Another important commemorative site in Vietnam is the Cu Chi Tunnels, a vast network of underground tunnels used by the Viet Cong during the war to evade detection and launch guerrilla attacks against American and South Vietnamese forces. Today, the tunnels have been preserved as a historic site and tourist attraction, allowing visitors to explore the cramped and claustrophobic conditions endured by Vietnamese soldiers during the conflict.

In the United States, significant landmarks and memorials related to the Vietnam War include the Vietnam Veterans Memorial in Washington, D.C., which features a black granite wall inscribed with the names of more than 58,000 American service members who died in the war. Designed by Maya Lin and dedicated in 1982, the memorial serves as a powerful tribute to the sacrifices of those who served and sacrificed in Vietnam, providing a place of solace and remembrance for veterans and their families.

Ethical Considerations: Navigating the Complexities

While Vietnam War tourism offers valuable opportunities for education, commemoration, and reconciliation, it also raises important ethical considerations regarding the commodification of war-related experiences for tourism purposes. From the portrayal of war to the treatment of local communities, these ethical considerations must be carefully navigated to ensure that war tourism remains respectful, responsible, and ethical in its approach.

One of the key ethical considerations surrounding Vietnam War tourism is the portrayal of war and its impact on local communities. While war tourism offers valuable opportunities for visitors to learn about the history and legacy of the Vietnam War, it is important that these experiences are presented in a sensitive and respectful manner that honors the experiences of those who lived through the conflict. This includes acknowledging the suffering and trauma endured by Vietnamese civilians and soldiers, as well as the complexities of the war and its aftermath.

Another ethical consideration is the treatment of local communities and the impact of tourism on their lives and livelihoods. While war tourism can bring economic benefits to communities in Vietnam, it can also lead to exploitation, cultural appropriation, and environmental degradation if not managed responsibly. It is important that tourism operators and visitors alike respect the rights and dignity of local communities, engage in meaningful dialogue and exchange, and support initiatives that promote sustainable development and cultural preservation.

In addition to these ethical considerations, there are also questions about the commercialization of war-related experiences and the commodification of trauma for tourism purposes. While war tourism can provide valuable opportunities for education and commemoration, it is important that these experiences are not reduced to mere spectacles or entertainment, but rather are approached with empathy, humility, and respect for the dignity of those who lived through the conflict.

In Conclusion: Balancing Education, Commemoration, and Responsibility

Vietnam War tourism offers valuable opportunities for education, commemoration, and reconciliation, providing visitors with insights into the complexities of war and its impact on local communities and historical memory. However, it is important that war tourism is approached with sensitivity, responsibility, and ethical awareness, ensuring that it respects the dignity of those who lived through the conflict and honors the sacrifices of those who served and sacrificed in Vietnam. By navigating the complexities of war tourism with empathy, humility, and respect, we can ensure that it remains a meaningful and ethical way to engage with the history and legacy of the Vietnam War for generations to come.

Chapter 11: Diplomatic Aftermath

The Vietnam War had profound diplomatic repercussions that reverberated far beyond the borders of Vietnam, shaping American foreign policy in Southeast Asia and influencing regional dynamics for decades to come. In this chapter, we will analyze the impact of the Vietnam War on American foreign policy, examine the process of reconciliation between the United States and Vietnam, and discuss the broader geopolitical consequences of the conflict for Southeast Asia.

Diplomatic Repercussions: Shifting Foreign Policy in Southeast Asia and Beyond

The Vietnam War fundamentally altered American foreign policy in Southeast Asia and reshaped the geopolitical landscape of the region. The conflict, which pitted the United States against North Vietnam and the Viet Cong, marked a significant departure from America's previous containment strategy aimed at containing the spread of communism in the region.

The United States' intervention in Vietnam was motivated by a desire to prevent the spread of communism and uphold its commitments to its allies in Southeast Asia. However, the war proved to be a costly and protracted conflict that ultimately failed to achieve its objectives, leading to a reassessment of American foreign policy priorities in the region.

In the aftermath of the Vietnam War, the United States adopted a more pragmatic and multilateral approach to diplomacy in Southeast Asia, focusing on economic engagement, regional cooperation, and the promotion of democracy and human rights. This shift in foreign policy reflected a recognition of the limitations of military intervention and the need for a more nuanced and sustainable approach to addressing the root causes of instability and conflict in the region.

Reconciliation with Vietnam: Normalization of Relations

One of the most significant diplomatic developments to emerge from the aftermath of the Vietnam War was the normalization of relations between the United States and Vietnam. Despite decades of enmity and mistrust, the two former adversaries embarked on a path of reconciliation in the years following the end of the war, seeking to heal the wounds of the past and build a more constructive relationship based on mutual respect and cooperation.

The process of normalization began in earnest in the 1990s, with the lifting of the U.S. trade embargo against Vietnam in 1994 and the establishment of diplomatic relations between the two countries in 1995. These developments paved the way for increased economic, cultural, and diplomatic exchange between the United States and Vietnam, as well as greater cooperation on issues of mutual interest such as trade, security, and regional stability.

Despite lingering challenges and differences of opinion on issues such as human rights and political freedom, the normalization of relations between the United States and Vietnam has proven to be a transformative process that has helped to overcome the legacy of the Vietnam War and build a more constructive and forward-looking partnership between the two countries.

Regional Dynamics: Geopolitical Consequences for Southeast Asia

The Vietnam War had far-reaching geopolitical consequences for Southeast Asia, reshaping regional dynamics and influencing the trajectory of political development in countries throughout the region. The conflict heightened tensions between communist and non-communist states in Southeast Asia, leading to a polarization of political alignments and a deepening of ideological divisions.

One of the most significant consequences of the Vietnam War was the spread of communism in Southeast Asia, as the victory of the Vietnamese communists inspired communist insurgencies and movements in neighboring countries such as Laos and Cambodia. This led to further instability and conflict in the region, culminating in the rise of communist regimes in Laos and Cambodia and the subsequent bloodshed and suffering inflicted by the Khmer Rouge regime in Cambodia.

The Vietnam War also had a profound impact on the Association of Southeast Asian Nations (ASEAN), a regional organization established in 1967 to promote economic cooperation and political stability in Southeast Asia. The war served as a catalyst for closer cooperation among ASEAN member states, who sought to bolster their collective security in the face of growing communist influence in the region.

In conclusion, the Vietnam War had far-reaching diplomatic repercussions that reshaped American foreign policy in Southeast Asia and influenced regional dynamics for decades to come. Despite the human cost and political upheaval caused by the conflict, the normalization of relations between the United States and Vietnam has provided a foundation for greater cooperation and engagement in the years since, helping to overcome the legacy of the war and build a more stable and prosperous future for the people of Southeast Asia.

Chapter 12: Veterans' Perspectives

The Vietnam War left an indelible mark on the men and women who served in its ranks, shaping their lives in profound and lasting ways. In this chapter, we will share the perspectives of Vietnam veterans on their experiences during and after the war, explore the challenges of reintegration they faced upon returning home, and highlight the ongoing advocacy efforts of veterans' organizations to address their needs and support their well-being.

Voices of Veterans: Stories from the Frontlines

The voices of Vietnam veterans provide a powerful and poignant window into the realities of war and its impact on those who served. From the jungles of Vietnam to the streets of American cities, these men and women bore witness to the horrors of combat, the camaraderie of brotherhood, and the trauma of war that would stay with them long after the guns fell silent.

For many Vietnam veterans, the experience of war was both harrowing and transformative, testing their courage, resilience, and humanity in ways they could never have imagined. From the chaos and confusion of battle to the quiet moments of reflection and camaraderie in between, their stories offer a glimpse into the full spectrum of human emotion and experience in the crucible of conflict.

Some veterans speak of the bonds forged in the heat of battle, the unbreakable ties of brotherhood that sustained them through the darkest days of war. Others recount the horrors of combat, the fear and uncertainty that haunted their every step, and the pain and loss of losing comrades in arms. Each story is unique, yet all share a common thread of sacrifice, courage, and resilience in the face of adversity.

Challenges of Reintegration: The Long Road

Home

For many Vietnam veterans, the end of the war marked the beginning of a new battle – the struggle to reintegrate into civilian life and rebuild their lives in the aftermath of conflict. Returning home after months or years of service in Vietnam, veterans faced a host of challenges, from finding employment and housing to dealing with physical and psychological wounds that would linger long after the war had ended.

One of the biggest challenges veterans faced upon returning home was the lack of understanding and support from the civilian population, many of whom viewed Vietnam veterans with suspicion, hostility, or indifference. The divisive nature of the war, coupled with widespread protests and anti-war sentiment, created a hostile and unwelcoming environment for returning veterans, many of whom felt isolated and alienated from the society they had fought to defend.

In addition to the social and cultural challenges of reintegration, Vietnam veterans also struggled to access the healthcare and support services they needed to address the physical and psychological wounds of war. For many veterans, the scars of Vietnam – both seen and unseen – would continue to haunt them long after the war had ended, affecting their physical health, mental well-being, and overall quality of life.

Continuing Advocacy: Fighting for Recognition and Support

Despite the challenges they faced, Vietnam veterans refused to be forgotten or ignored, banding together to advocate for their rights and demand the recognition and support they deserved. Through grassroots organizing, lobbying efforts, and public awareness campaigns, veterans' organizations such as the Vietnam Veterans of America (VVA), the Disabled American Veterans (DAV), and the Vietnam Veterans Memorial Fund (VVMF) worked tirelessly to raise awareness about the needs of Vietnam veterans and ensure they received the care and support they needed to rebuild their lives.

One of the most significant victories for Vietnam veterans came in 1982 with the dedication of the Vietnam Veterans Memorial in Washington, D.C. Designed by Maya Lin, the memorial features a black granite wall inscribed with the names of more than 58,000 Americans who died in the war, providing a place of solace and remembrance for veterans and their families. The memorial served as a powerful symbol of the sacrifices made by Vietnam veterans and helped to heal the wounds of war that had divided the nation for so long.

In addition to the Vietnam Veterans Memorial, Vietnam veterans also fought for and won important legislative victories that expanded access to healthcare, disability benefits, and other support services for veterans and their families. The passage of the Agent Orange Act of 1991, the Veterans Health Care Eligibility Reform Act of 1996, and the Veterans Millennium Health Care and Benefits Act of 1999 represented significant milestones in the ongoing effort to address the needs of Vietnam veterans and ensure they received the care and support they deserved.

In Conclusion: Honoring the Legacy of Service

The voices of Vietnam veterans offer a powerful reminder of the sacrifices made by those who served in the war and the ongoing struggles they faced upon returning home. From the jungles of Vietnam to the halls of Congress, Vietnam veterans fought bravely and tirelessly to ensure their sacrifices were remembered and honored, advocating for the recognition and support they deserved.

As we reflect on the legacy of Vietnam veterans, it is important to recognize the debt of gratitude we owe them for their service and sacrifice. By honoring their stories, supporting their needs, and remembering their contributions, we can ensure that the legacy of

Vietnam veterans lives on for generations to come, inspiring us to strive for a more just, compassionate, and inclusive society for all.

Chapter 13: War and Memory

The Vietnam War occupies a unique place in American collective memory, its legacy shaped by decades of reflection, commemoration, and debate. In this chapter, we will examine how the Vietnam War is remembered and commemorated in American society, discuss controversies surrounding the construction and preservation of memorials dedicated to the conflict, and explore how memories of the war are passed down through families and communities.

Collective Memory: Remembering Vietnam

The Vietnam War remains one of the most divisive and controversial conflicts in American history, its legacy deeply etched into the national consciousness and cultural landscape. For many Americans, the war evokes memories of protest and dissent, sacrifice and heroism, trauma and healing – a complex tapestry of emotions and experiences that continues to shape how the conflict is remembered and understood.

One of the most enduring symbols of the Vietnam War is the Vietnam Veterans Memorial in Washington, D.C., commonly known as "The Wall." Designed by Maya Lin and dedicated in 1982, the memorial consists of two black granite walls inscribed with the names of more than 58,000 Americans who died in the war, providing a solemn and reflective space for remembrance and mourning. For many visitors, The Wall serves as a powerful reminder of the human cost of war and a place of pilgrimage for veterans, their families, and others seeking to pay their respects and honor the sacrifices made by those who served.

In addition to The Wall, the Vietnam War is also remembered and commemorated in a variety of other ways, including through books, films, documentaries, art exhibits, and educational programs. These diverse forms of cultural expression offer insights into the complexities of the war and its impact on American society and culture, providing opportunities for reflection, dialogue, and healing for those who lived through the conflict and those who came after.

Memorialization Controversies: Debates Over Memory and Meaning

Despite its widespread popularity and acclaim, the Vietnam Veterans Memorial has not been without controversy, with debates over memory and meaning continuing to shape how the conflict is remembered and commemorated in American society. One of the most contentious issues surrounding the memorial is the way in which it represents the war and its veterans, with critics arguing that its minimalist design fails to adequately convey the complexity and diversity of the Vietnam experience.

Another source of controversy is the inclusion of the names of Vietnamese civilians and soldiers on The Wall, a decision that sparked heated debate among veterans, policymakers, and the public. While some saw it as a gesture of reconciliation and recognition of the shared sacrifice made by both Americans and Vietnamese, others viewed it as inappropriate and disrespectful to the memory of American servicemen and women who died in the conflict.

In addition to debates over the design and content of memorials, controversies have also arisen over efforts to preserve and protect existing memorials dedicated to the Vietnam War. In recent years, there have been concerns about the condition of The Wall and other Vietnam War memorials, with some critics arguing that they have been neglected or forgotten by the government and the public, underscoring the need for ongoing efforts to ensure their long-term preservation and maintenance.

Intergenerational Transmission: Passing Down Memories of War

Memories of the Vietnam War are not confined to the past – they are passed down through families and communities, shaping the identities and perspectives of future generations. For the children and grandchildren of Vietnam veterans, the war is not just a historical event but a lived experience, a legacy that continues to influence their lives and worldviews in profound and often unexpected ways.

One way in which memories of the Vietnam War are transmitted intergenerationally is through family stories and personal narratives, as veterans share their experiences and reflections with their loved ones. These stories, often tinged with pain and pride, provide a window into the realities of war and the enduring impact it has had on those who served and their families.

In addition to family stories, memories of the Vietnam War are also passed down through cultural representations and collective rituals of remembrance, such as Memorial Day ceremonies, Veterans Day parades, and community events honoring veterans and their service. These rituals serve as opportunities for reflection, solidarity, and healing, allowing individuals and communities to come together to honor the sacrifices made by those who served and to ensure that their memory lives on for future generations.

In Conclusion: The Power of Memory

The Vietnam War may be a distant memory for some, but its legacy continues to reverberate through American society and culture, shaping how we remember and understand the conflict and its impact on those who served and sacrificed. From The Wall to family stories passed down through generations, memories of Vietnam are a testament to the enduring power of remembrance and the human capacity for resilience, healing, and reconciliation in the face of war and its aftermath.

As we reflect on the legacy of the Vietnam War and its place in American memory, it is important to recognize the diversity of experiences and perspectives that define how the conflict is remembered and commemorated. By honoring the sacrifices made by those who served and ensuring that their memory lives on for future generations, we can ensure that the lessons of Vietnam are not forgotten and that the human cost of war is never taken for granted.

Chapter 14: Lessons for the Future

The Vietnam War stands as a sobering reminder of the complexities and consequences of armed conflict, offering valuable lessons that continue to resonate in the 21st century. In this chapter, we will reflect on the enduring relevance of the Vietnam War for contemporary challenges and conflicts, discuss the ethical considerations and moral obligations involved in decisions to intervene militarily, and explore strategies for building a more peaceful world in the face of global insecurity and uncertainty.

Revisiting the Lessons of Vietnam: Applying Historical Insights to Contemporary Challenges

The Vietnam War remains a touchstone for policymakers, scholars, and citizens alike, its legacy serving as a cautionary tale of the perils of interventionism, the limitations of military power, and the importance of understanding the complexities of conflict and its root causes. As we grapple with contemporary challenges such as terrorism, insurgency, and state fragility, the lessons of Vietnam offer valuable insights into the complexities of modern warfare and the challenges of achieving sustainable peace and security in an increasingly interconnected world.

One of the key lessons of Vietnam is the importance of understanding the historical, political, and cultural context of conflict, and the dangers of intervening in conflicts without a clear understanding of the complexities and dynamics at play. The Vietnam War was characterized by a lack of clarity and consensus about the objectives and strategies of American intervention, leading to a protracted and ultimately unsuccessful conflict that claimed the lives of millions of people and left lasting scars on American society and global politics.

Another lesson of Vietnam is the importance of humility and restraint in the exercise of military power, and the recognition that military intervention should always be a last resort, pursued only when all diplomatic, economic, and other non-military means have been exhausted. The Vietnam War demonstrated the dangers of hubris and overconfidence in military solutions, and the need for policymakers to carefully weigh the costs and consequences of intervention against the potential benefits and risks.

The Human Cost of War: Ethical Considerations and Moral Obligations

One of the most profound and enduring lessons of Vietnam is the human cost of war, and the ethical considerations and moral obligations involved in decisions to intervene militarily. The Vietnam War was marked by widespread human rights abuses, atrocities, and systemic failures of leadership and policy, resulting in the loss of millions of lives and the displacement of millions more.

As we confront contemporary conflicts and crises, it is imperative that we remember the human toll of war and the responsibility we bear to protect and uphold the rights and dignity of all people, regardless of nationality, ethnicity, or religion. The Vietnam War serves as a stark reminder of the horrors of war and the importance of upholding international humanitarian law and norms, including the prohibition against genocide, crimes against humanity, and war crimes.

Another ethical consideration raised by the Vietnam War is the principle of proportionality, which holds that the use of force must be proportionate to the threat posed and the objectives sought, and that the benefits of military action must outweigh the costs in terms of human suffering and destruction. The Vietnam War raised profound questions about the proportionality of American intervention, and the moral implications of pursuing military objectives at the expense of civilian lives and livelihoods.

Building a More Peaceful World: Strategies for Conflict Resolution and International Cooperation

Despite the enduring legacy of the Vietnam War, there is reason for hope that the lessons of the past can inform a more peaceful and just future. As we confront the myriad challenges of the 21st century – from terrorism and nuclear proliferation to climate change and pandemics – it is imperative that we learn from the mistakes of the past and work together to build a more peaceful and prosperous world for all.

One of the key strategies for conflict resolution and international cooperation is diplomacy, dialogue, and negotiation, which offer a peaceful and constructive alternative to armed conflict and coercion. The Vietnam War demonstrated the limitations of military force as a means of achieving lasting peace and stability, and the importance of engaging in meaningful dialogue and negotiation to address the root causes of conflict and build sustainable peace.

Another strategy for building a more peaceful world is the promotion of democracy, human rights, and the rule of law, which serve as essential foundations for peace, stability, and prosperity. The Vietnam War highlighted the dangers of authoritarianism, repression, and political instability, and the importance of supporting democratic governance and respect for human rights as essential pillars of a just and peaceful world order.

In addition to diplomacy and democracy, international cooperation and collective action are also critical for addressing global challenges and advancing common interests and values. The Vietnam War underscored the interconnectedness of the world and the need for countries to work together to address shared challenges such as poverty, inequality, and environmental degradation, and to build a more just, sustainable, and inclusive world for future generations.

In Conclusion: Learning from the Past, Working Towards a Better Future

The lessons of the Vietnam War are as relevant today as they were half a century ago, offering valuable insights into the complexities and consequences of armed conflict and the challenges of building a more peaceful and just world. As we confront the myriad challenges of the 21st century, it is imperative that we learn from the mistakes of the past and work together to

Chapter 15: Conclusion

As we reach the conclusion of our exploration into the Vietnam War and its enduring legacies, it's crucial to reflect on the key themes and insights that have emerged throughout this book. We've journeyed through the complexities of the conflict, delved into its human costs and diplomatic repercussions, and examined its profound impact on American society, culture, and memory. Now, let's summarize these key themes, consider the ongoing significance of the Vietnam War, and offer final reflections on the importance of grappling with the complexities of war, memory, and reconciliation in shaping a more peaceful world.

Summarizing Key Themes and Insights

Throughout this book, we've encountered a multitude of themes and insights that have shed light on the Vietnam War and its aftermath. From the roots of the conflict to the experiences of soldiers on the frontlines, from the societal divisions at home to the diplomatic repercussions abroad, we've witnessed the far-reaching impact of the war on individuals, communities, and nations. Key themes include:

1. Historical Context: Understanding the historical, political, and cultural factors that contributed to the outbreak of the Vietnam War, including colonialism, nationalism, and the Cold War dynamics.

2. Human Cost: Examining the profound toll of the war in terms of casualties, both civilian and military, and the long-lasting physical, psychological, and environmental consequences.

3. Social Impact: Exploring the societal divisions caused by the war, including protests, draft resistance, and the counterculture movement, and the role of media in shaping public opinion and government policy.

4. Veterans' Experiences: Sharing the personal narratives of Vietnam veterans, their challenges of reintegration into civilian life, and their ongoing advocacy efforts for recognition and support.

5. Diplomatic Aftermath: Analyzing the impact of the war on American foreign policy in Southeast Asia and beyond, the process of reconciliation with Vietnam, and the broader geopolitical consequences for the region.

6. Memorialization and Memory: Examining how the war is remembered and commemorated in American society, controversies surrounding memorials, and the intergenerational transmission of memories of war.

Looking Ahead: The Ongoing Significance of the Vietnam War

Despite the passage of time, the Vietnam War continues to hold profound significance for future generations of Americans and people around the world. Its lessons – both painful and poignant – serve as a cautionary tale for policymakers, scholars, and citizens alike, reminding us of the human costs of war and the imperative of pursuing peace through diplomacy, dialogue, and cooperation.

As we confront the challenges of the 21st century – from terrorism and nuclear proliferation to climate change and pandemics – the lessons of Vietnam offer valuable insights into the complexities of conflict and the importance of understanding its root causes and dynamics. By learning from the mistakes of the past and working together to build a more just, peaceful, and sustainable world, we can honor the sacrifices made by those who served and ensure that their memory lives on for generations to come.

Final Reflections: Grappling with the Complexities of War, Memory, and Reconciliation

As we close this chapter and this book, it's essential to acknowledge the complexity and nuance of the Vietnam War and its legacies. War is not just a series of battles and strategies – it is a deeply human experience, marked by sacrifice, suffering, and resilience. By grappling with the complexities of war, memory, and reconciliation, we honor the experiences of those who lived through the conflict and strive to build a more peaceful and just world for future generations.

In our increasingly interconnected and uncertain world, the lessons of Vietnam remain as relevant as ever. We must confront the realities of war with courage and humility, recognizing the human cost of conflict and the moral imperative of pursuing peace through dialogue, understanding, and compassion. By engaging with the stories and experiences of those who lived through the Vietnam War, we can gain a deeper appreciation for the complexities of the past and the possibilities for a more hopeful future.

In closing, let us remember the words of Maya Lin, designer of the Vietnam Veterans Memorial: "It is important that we never forget the sacrifices made by those who served in Vietnam, and that we continue to honor their memory in the years to come." May we carry forward the lessons and legacies of the Vietnam War with humility, empathy, and a commitment to building a world where peace prevails and the wounds of war are healed.

Don't miss out!

Visit the website below and you can sign up to receive emails whenever MICHAEL SMITH publishes a new book. There's no charge and no obligation.

https://books2read.com/r/B-A-RBLKB-PNKHD

BOOKS2READ

Connecting independent readers to independent writers.

Also by MICHAEL SMITH

America Literature 20th century
Dictatorship Diaries
Vietnam War Echoes

About the Author

Michael Smith, an American literature scholar, holds a Ph.D. in English Literature and teaches at the university level. With a focus on American literary tradition, Smith's engaging prose and scholarly insight have graced academic journals and literary magazines. He explores diverse voices and themes in American literature, from classics to contemporary works. Smith's passion for storytelling extends beyond academia, inspiring readers to appreciate the depth and complexity of American letters.